You Cut Your Engines and Let Yourself Be Pulled into the Hole by the Tremendous Gravity Field.

Like a speck down a swirling black drain, you plunge into the void . . . Gravity increases till you feel as if you will be crushed . . . You fear that your ship is on the verge of coming apart. You stagger to the control panel and then pause. Do you dare restart the engines? A start-up now could empty you into almost any place and any time. The other option is to hold on for a few more parsecs and hope to break out of the hole safe and at the correct destination.

If you want to risk a restart and take your chances on your destination, turn to page 20.

If you elect to try to hold on in hopes that the ship doesn't blow, then turn to page 18.

REMEMBER—*YOU* MAKE THE LIFE-OR-DEATH DECISIONS!

WHICH WAY BOOKS for you to enjoy

WHICH WAY BOOKS *11

SPACE RAIDERS AND THE PLANET OF DOOM

Stephen Mooser

Illustrated by Gordon Tomei

AN ARCHWAY PAPERBACK
Published by POCKET BOOKS • NEW YORK

AN ARCHWAY PAPERBACK *Original*

An Archway Paperback published by
POCKET BOOKS, a division of Simon & Schuster, Inc.
1230 Avenue of the Americas, New York, N.Y. 10020

ISBN: 0-671-46732-8

First Archway Paperback printing August, 1983

10 9 8 7 6 5 4 3 2 1

Attention!

Which Way Books must be read in a special way. DO NOT READ THE PAGES IN ORDER. If you do, the story will make no sense at all. Instead, follow the directions at the bottom of each page until you come to an ending. Only then should you return to the beginning and start over again, making different choices this time.

There are many possibilities for exciting adventures. Some of the endings are good; some of the endings are bad. If you meet a terrible fate, you can reverse it in your next story by making new choices.

Remember: Follow the directions carefully and have fun!

You are the young assistant in a small, cluttered office on Hegel, fourth planet in the Centaurus system. On the door outside a sign says: QUASAR GALACTIC SALVAGE SERVICE. Above your desk is posted the company slogan: YOU WRECK IT—WE COLLECT IT. It's summer and everyone is on vacation. So, for the time being, you're in charge.

At the moment you're plotting out your next job, the recovery of a tri-clenium cruiser that crashed on a small, unnamed planet in the Delta Quadrant. She was carrying a load of diloid crystals, the most powerful substance in the universe. Your only competition will be the infamous Tentacles Shiver, gangleader of a ruthless band of galactic outlaws known as the Space Raiders. Tentacles, a six-foot mutant jellyfish who walks on his long tentacles, emerged from a radioactive ocean some twenty years earlier. Since then Shiver has spent part of his time assembling his grotesque gang and the other part pillaging and enslaving whole planets throughout the galaxy. Tentacles wants the crystals in order to further his dream of dominating the universe. Your job will be to beat him to the wreck and recover the crystals for yourself.

(continued on page 2)

Just as you are about to board your ship a friend runs up with some startling news.

"The *Nova Princess* is down and abandoned. She's open for salvage."

"The *Princess!*" you exclaim. "She was carrying the Millennium Device. Is it safe?"

"Hardly," says your friend. "One of the crew members went nuts and programmed it to go off in a week. The only way it can be deactivated is by solving some difficult riddles."

"Where is that crew member now?" you ask.

"Disappeared—along with the rest of the crew. The Federation is offering a billion drams of gold to whomever can shut off the device."

"If that thing isn't deactivated that whole end of the galaxy could blow," you say.

"And that just could happen because she's down on the most dreaded planet in the universe. The place from which no one has ever returned," she says.

You know at once your friend can be talking about only one place—the Planet of Doom.

"Well, what's it going to be?" she asks. "Tentacles or . . . Doom?"

If you take on Tentacles and try to get the crystals, turn to page 5.

If you want your next stop to be the Planet of Doom, turn to page 3.

With the double moons of Hegel high over-head you board your ship and lift off for the Planet of Doom. Before long you've accelerated to the speed of light. Then, passing your hand over a green sensor on your control panel, you make the jump into hyperspace and roar away into the lightless void at quantum speeds.

You turn control of the ship over to your onboard computer and settle down to reviewing a report on the Millennium Device, the powerful bomb you must deactivate once you reach your destination.

You're barely halfway through the report when your computer sends you an urgent message:

SALVAGE ALERT! SALVAGE ALERT! IN THREE PARSECS WE WILL BE PASSING OVER THE PLANET ARACHNIA IN THE RAGON SYSTEM. I HAVE DETECTED A LARGE DESPOSIT OF RARE FORTY-POUND BOROLITE EMERALDS ON THE SURFACE. DO YOU WISH TO BREAK HYPER-SPACE IN ORDER TO RECOVER THE GEMS?

You bet you do! Borolite emeralds of that size could be worth a fortune.

You pull your ship off automatic pilot and break from hyperspace in a blinding flash of gold and purple light.

(continued on page 4)

You flip on your viewscreen and look down on the brown planet of Arachnia. Your scanner locates the emeralds and hypermagnification brings them into focus. They lie on a barren, rocky plain and seem to be tangled in a mass of white ropes. Further scanning locates the planet's only life forms, a nest of giant, four-hundred-pound spiders in a cave some three kilometers away.

The spiders don't appear to be a threat at that distance, so you set down your ship. After a quick survey you head for the emeralds. There's something about the tangle of white ropes around the jewels that fascinates you. It's not their glistening appearance; rather, it's their honeylike smell. Before long your mouth is watering. You've got to have a taste of whatever it is that's coating the rope. You well know rule number six in the Uniform Space Code of Conduct: "Never taste or touch a thing until it's gone through poison analysis."

"But how," you wonder, "could anything that smells so good possibly be bad?"

The poison analyzer is back at the ship, and anyway, all you want is one tiny little taste.

If you decide to return for the analyzer, then go to page 11.

If you want to taste the sweet substance on the rope at once, then turn to page 8.

You lift off from Hegel and head for the nearest Stargate, a black hole that bends space and time and can shuttle you to your destination in minutes. However, when you arrive above the Stargate you notice that the hole is rotating. All space jockeys know that a rotating black hole can be as dangerous to enter as a pit full of snakes. It could send you to your correct destination, but then it might just as well toss you out into another time, or even another universe. The crystals you hope to salvage won't wait forever and the nearest alternate Stargate is days away.

If you choose to take your chance in the black hole, turn to page 17.

If you want to play it safe and travel to another shuttle point, turn to page 6.

You bring your ship about and program your onboard computer for the Delta Quadrant. At sublight speed it will take you almost a week to reach your destination—that is, if nothing goes wrong.

But something does go wrong. Two days out you encounter a strange cloud of highly ionized gas. Your sensors are unable to penetrate the gas, so you have no idea what awaits you inside. You do know that to avoid the cloud will delay your arrival by a full day, and for all you know Tentacles is already on the scene salvaging the crystals.

If you decide to save time by going through the cloud, turn to page 21.

If you want to avoid trouble and circle around the cloud, go to page 9.

You return to the ship and rummage through your closets looking for the poison analyzer.

"Why do I have to be such a slob?" you say to yourself. "This place is such a mess I can never find anything when I want it."

After what seems like hours you finally locate the analyzer.

"Now, at last," you say. "I'm going to be able to try that delicious honey."

Suddenly you hear a knock at the door.

"Who's there?" you ask.

When you get no reply you step to the door.

"Who's there?" you ask again. And again you are answered by silence.

If you want to open the door, turn to page 38.

If you want to go upstairs and check out the visitor on the viewscreen, turn to page 11.

You have to have a taste of that Arachnian honey. You decide to scoop up a bit of the sweet nectar with your hand, but the second your finger hits the sticky substance you make a frightening discovery. It's not honey at all, but some sort of superglue and you've been instantly cemented to the rope.

You've fallen into a perfectly set trap. Suddenly everything begins to become clear in your mind. The ropes are not really ropes but a web, and the emeralds, which are probably fakes, are the bait that lures victims into the trap.

You look up at the distant hills and gulp. Two four-hundred-pound spiders have just charged out of a dark cave and are racing towards you in a dusty stampede. With your free hand you fish out a laser knife and flip it open. You slice through the web and step away from the emeralds, dragging a twenty-meter hunk of the sticky rope behind you.

If you want to make a run for the ship, turn to page 39.

If you elect to make a stand, turn to page 14.

You bank around the strange cloud and resume your journey. Nearly a week later you reach your destination and head down toward the small, rocky planet that holds the remains of the tri-clenium cruiser and its precious cargo. As you near touchdown you see six or seven small figures shuttling between the wreck and another, smaller ship.

"What rotten luck," you mutter. "Universal Space Law gives the rights of salvage to those reaching the wreck first."

If you decide to abandon the salvage and head, instead, for your other assignment on the Planet of Doom, turn to page 3.

If you decide to land anyway and meet the aliens, turn to page 10.

You set down not far from the alien craft and approach cautiously. The aliens you had spotted earlier turn out to be robots; at least, that's what they appear to be from a distance. Close up, however, you detect a certain human quality in their violet eyes.

You take out your photon pistol but keep it pointed at the ground. One of the robots approaches and reaches for the pistol. You quickly size up the situation. It's six against one. The odds don't look good, and they'd be even worse without the weapon.

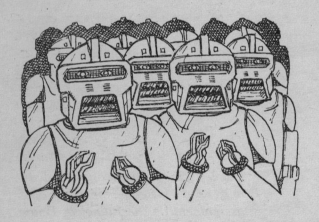

If you choose to give up your gun, go to page 12.

If you elect to fire, turn to page 35.

You flip on the viewscreen and scan the outside of the ship. What you see disgusts and frightens you at the same time. There, clambering about your ship, is a huge four-hundred-pound spider. While you watch she spins a thick, white web about your ship. You groan. Its clear your hairy-legged friend intends for you to stay awhile.

"I bet those emeralds were nothing but a trap to lure me here," you say to yourself. "I'm afraid that spider I'm up against is no dummy."

Luckily you're no dummy either.

You kick off your shoes and step onto a rubber pad near the control panel. Then you twist a dial and send a thousand volts of electricity through the skin of the ship. The pad protects you, but there is no protection for the spider. You hear a high-pitched shriek and then see her drop to the ground and skitter away.

A few moments later you've blasted off the surface of Arachnia and resumed your journey to Doom.

"I'm glad to be rid of that spider," you say, accelerating once more to superlight speed. "Anything with more than four legs always gives me the creeps."

Now go to page 16.

The robot takes the gun from your hand, casually transfers it to his mouth—and eats it! When he sees the shocked expression on your face he quickly explains, "I'm sorry, I thought you were offering me a bite to eat. We are Hubots with human minds implanted in robot bodies. We exist on a diet of steel and copper. In fact, that's what brought us here. The cruiser here has been a wonderful snack. Care to join us?"

"No, thanks," you reply. "Actually, I was more interested in the cargo of crystals."

"You eat crystals?" asks a Hubot.

"No, let's just say I collect them," you explain. "Would you mind if I took the crystals? I promise I won't touch a piece of metal."

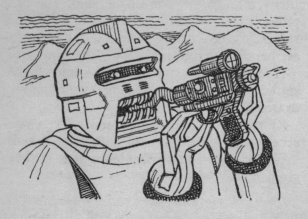

(continued on page 13)

"Be our guest," says one of the Hubots, "but before you step inside that ship I should warn you that it's not very safe. We've sucked out all the bolts. It could collapse at any moment."

You glance uneasily at the heavens. Tentacles could be arriving in his ship, the *Raider's Revenge,* at any moment.

"If you'll wait a day or two we'll eat our way to your crystals," says one of the robots. "Why take a chance on getting hurt?"

If you decide to try for the crystals now even though the cruiser is dangerous to enter, turn to page 41.

If you choose to wait till the Hubots eat their way to the crystals, turn to page 50.

With a twenty-foot section of web still stuck to your hand, you take a deep breath and turn to face the stampeding spiders. You once saw a movie in which a woman roped two cows at once and you're tempted to stop the hairy creatures in a similar way, if you can.

Turn to page 32.

You head off down one of the Wumpus tunnels. You've only gone a short distance when you come to a brightly painted door. Above the door are the words PROFESSOR CHORTLE. On the door itself is a sign saying, "Come Inside and See the Largest Diamond in the Universe."

"That I have to see," you say to yourself.

To see it you must go to page 57.

Your voyage is relatively uneventful until you are almost to Doom. In a zone in which there should not be as much as a speck of cosmic dust, your EWI (Early Warning Interceptors) have detected large chunks of debris. In hyperspace an encounter with any solid object could be fatal. You realize you must break to sublight speed at once. You reach for the throttle and begin to pull it back. It comes halfway—and then sticks!

Your EWI signals that you are just ten parsecs from encountering the debris. In a near panic you reach for a hammer, then hesitate.

"Maybe I should give it one last pull with my hands," you think. "I'd hate to break off the throttle trying to hammer it free."

SIX PARSECS TO ACT.

No time to try both.

If you use the hammer to knock the throttle loose, turn to page 30.

If you pull it again with your hands, using all your strength, turn to page 33.

You cut your engines and let yourself be pulled into the hole by the tremendous gravity field. Like a speck down a swirling black drain you plunge into the void. Time slows. Colors, many in the ultraviolet range, pulsate around you. Gravity increases till you feel as if you will be crushed. You've never experienced such strong gravity forces and you fear that your ship is on the verge of coming apart. You stagger to the control panel and then pause. Do you dare restart the engines? A start-up now could empty you into almost any place and any time. The other option is to hold on for a few more parsecs and hope to break out of the hole safe and at the correct destination.

If you want to risk a restart and take your chances on your destination, turn to page 20.

If you elect to try to hold on in hopes that the ship doesn't blow, turn to page 18.

The gravity forces increase. You feel as if you are being squeezed out of a six-inch tube. You gasp for breath, slip to your knees. Then, suddenly, everything is brilliant white. You've exploded out of the hole. A quick glance at the stars on your viewscreen confirms that you've emerged into the Delta Quadrant. You fire your thrusters and bring your ship around 90 degrees. A small, rocky planet, the final resting place of the tri-clenium cruiser, rises up on the horizon. Suddenly a proton fireball cuts across your bow and explodes. On your viewscreen a red and black jellyfish-shaped craft hoves into sight. One look at the laughing shark painted on its side tells you all you need to know. It's the *Raider's Revenge*, an outlaw star cruiser under the command of Tentacles Shiver. Pow! Another proton blast rattles your ship.

(continued on page 19)

You lock onto the *Revenge*'s control room and your screen fills with the quivering blob known as Tentacles Shiver.

"Surrender!" he bellows. "Give up and I'll spare your ship. If you leave the crystals to me you'll be free to go." Then, waving one of his tentacles, he adds, "Resist and I'll blast you into quarks. Quickly now, what'll it be?"

You gulp. You know you're locked in his sights. But to abandon the crystals is to doom the galaxy to Shiver's dictatorship.

If you decide to give up the crystals to save your life, turn to page 117.

If you want to try to resist, turn to page 37.

You power up your thrusters and catch the edge of the black hole like a surfer ducking under the curl. Then you slam the throttle forward and kick free of the hole's tremendous gravity. When you break out you find yourself in a universe that looks strangely familar and yet somewhat alien. You think you've seen the stars before, but they appear to be out of place. Within the quadrant you locate two planets, one green, the other blue. Before long your tri-space coordinator has pinpointed your location in time and space. The place is the Omega-three Quadrant. The planets are known as Fuego and Koren. The time is 75 million years—in the past!

You sink to your seat. "Blast!" you mutter. "I'm trapped in time."

If you decide to explore the green planet, turn to page 29.

If you elect to go down to the blue planet, turn to page 25.

You hold your breath as you plunge into the mysterious cloud. You feel as if you're in a huge neon tube. Red and green bolts of charged ions crash against your ship. You look around the room and are suddenly struck by a horrible feeling of dread. Everything has been reversed! Everything is backward, from the writing on the walls to your reflection in the mirror. You've entered a cloud of anti-ions. The controls have been so scrambled there is no saving the ship. You grab the communicator and make a last desperate plea for help, but no one understands your dying cries of *Pleh! Pleh! Pleh!*

The End

You slow the ship to a bare crawl. Even at such a reduced speed a brush with one of those giant rocks could split your ship wide open.

Just then you see a wondrous sight. It's a school of space dolphins, thousands of them. Except for their habitat they are almost identical to sea dolphins. They cruise the cosmos seeking out their favorite food, cosmic dust, which they strain through special filters in their mouths.

Any other time you would have been glad to see these gentle creatures, but right now they are the last thing you want crowding around your ship. You need all the room you can get in order to maneuver through the rocks. Your ship is equipped with a sonic screamer that can emit high-pitched sounds in the ultra range. Turning on the screamer will surely drive the sharp-eared dolphins away. You hate to send them off, but you can't tolerate any further delay.

If you decide to drive away the dolphins with the screamer, turn to page 27.

If you want to let the dolphins stick around, turn to page 26.

"What's this?" you ask, donning the cape.

"It's a self-contained refrigeration unit," explains one of the creatures, who identifies herself as Lorinda. "All us Fuegans wear them. Ever since our planet shifted orbit we've suffered terrible heat. Those of us who are left live underground now. We wear these whenever we near the surface."

"Even underground living will be impossible in another week or two," says Gall, the other Fuegan. "Please take us with you in your ship."

"How many of you are there?" you ask.

"Nearly fifty," says Lorinda.

"I'm sorry, but I couldn't get off the ground with a load like that," you say.

"Please," they beg. "Please save our lives."

If you agree to take them with you, turn to page 84.

If you decide your ship will crash if it has to carry the Fuegans, turn to page 89.

You glide down over the steaming jungles of the planet named Koren. You remember this place from your history books, a planet that closely resembles earth in geography and history. Like earth, it had a highly advanced civilization that destroyed itself in one of the galaxy's first nuclear wars. But, of course, that was recently. This is the Koren of 75 million years ago.

You swoop down to a small clearing and land. Before leaving your ship you begin a survey of the area. Your sensors detect a large dinosaur in the area. They also detect the presence of a small animal, a saber-toothed tiger cub. He's dangerously close to a bubbling mass of tar.

If you decide to dash out of the ship to shoo the cub away from the tar, turn to page 48.

If you choose to stay inside till your survey is complete, turn to page 64.

The dolphins crowd around your ship, nearly bringing it to a standstill.

"I've got to get going," you think to yourself. "The galaxy is depending on me to defuse the Millennium Device."

All at once you hear a voice inside your head. Someone is speaking to you telepathically.

"Just follow us," says the voice. "We'll guide you through the rocks."

You glance out the viewscreen and see one of the dolphins wagging his tail at you. "It's okay," says the voice again. "We'll take good care of you."

"Well, I'll be an android's uncle!" you exclaim. "I had always heard that dolphins were smart, but I didn't realize they were telepathic."

You give an okay sign to the dolphin and turn up your engines. Then you follow his lead as he takes you through the maze of rocks and boulders that litter your path. Within a few hours you have emerged on the far side of the rock field.

"I can't thank you enough," you tell your guides.

"We're just glad we could have been of assistance," comes back the telepathic reply.

Now on to your mission. Doom awaits you.

Indeed it does. Please turn to page 28.

You haven't turned on your sonic screamer since you used it to trigger an avalanche on the ice planet Glacius, and you don't like using it now; but the dolphins have so crowded the ship that you've been brought to a standstill.

"Sorry, fellows," you say, turning the screamer up to 6.3 in the ultra range, "but I've got to get going."

Within moments the screamer has done its job. The dolphins scatter from the painful waves and disappear into the cosmos as silently and smoothly as they arrived.

All at once a sudden jolt focuses your attention on the task at hand: navigating through the rocky remains of the Planet Obon.

Bam! Another rock, this one the size of a skyscraper, tumbles onto your ship. Too late you realize why the dolphins appeared in the first place. They wanted to guide you safely out of danger. For centuries sea dolphins have guided ships through rocky straits, and space dolphins have been known to do the same thing.

Bam! Crash! Crunch! Three more rocks bounce off the thin shell of your ship. You cut the sonic screamer, but it's too late. The dolphins are long gone and so, apparently, are your chances of getting through the rock field in one piece.

Bam! Crunch! Pow!

The End

Before your day is out you arrive above your destination, the dreaded Planet of Doom. Looking down from your orbit all you can see is a small planet shrouded in a thick layer of smoke. The atmosphere is so dense that not even your sensors can penetrate it.

"For all I know the ground there is afire," you say. "That could be why no one has ever returned from Doom."

You admit that a landing would be risky, but, at the same time, you know it will be impossible to find the Nova Princess from orbit.

If you are afraid of landing and want, instead, to pursue your other mission, turn to page 6.

If you choose to risk a landing on Doom, turn to page 71.

When you finally arrive above Fuego you make a surprising discovery. White smoke-stacks, some hundreds of feet tall, protrude from the burnt green soil.

"Well, I'll be," you say. "Looks like there is intelligent life down there."

Before long you set down on the smooth surface of the planet and climb out of your ship. The outside temperature is unbearable, nearly 180 degrees. You make a frantic dash for the shade of a nearby cave. As you enter the cave you see two creatures wearing tent-like robes.

"Quickly," says one of the creatures, a short fellow with a face like a pig. "Put on this robe."

If you decide to flee to the ship, turn to page 31.

If you accept the robe, turn to page 24.

With but four parsecs to go you bang the throttle with the hammer. It doesn't budge, and now you have but two parsecs remaining. In desperation you pull back the hammer and smash the throttle stick with all your might. However, rather than breaking free it simply snaps in two. You reach for the broken stick, but it's already too late. You're in the danger zone.

Bam! You've struck something a glancing blow and the ship begins to tumble. Over and over you go, hopelessly, and helplessly, out of control.

You strap yourself into your seat and hold on. Your hammer has brought you a hyper-space amusement ride. But it's a ride you'd just as soon not be on, because there is no telling when it might be over, or where it might end up.

The End

"No, don't put me in that thing," you scream, racing from the cave and heading for the ship.

Halfway to safety you collapse from the terrible heat. By the time the aliens reach you you're suffering from an extreme case of heat-stroke.

"You shouldn't have run," says one of the creatures. "We only wanted to help."

You wish you could answer them, but you can't. Your brain has been toasted, and so all you can say in your delirium are snappy phrases like "blam, balla, baba" and "moo, gaga, dum."

The End

When the spiders are less than 100 meters away you begin to whirl the rope above your head. Right at the last you cut it free with your laser knife. Unleashed, it whips across the sands and wraps itself around the spiders' legs. In no time they're hopelessly tangled in their own sticky web.

"They'll be stuck for days," you think, smiling.

Before long you blast away from Arachnia and resume your superlight journey to Doom.

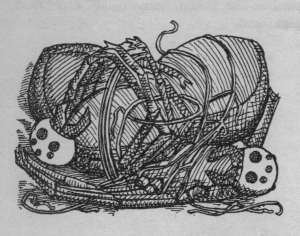

Now go to page 16.

You pull back on the stick with all your strength, but it still won't move. Four parsecs to go, and you elect to try another method of freeing the stick. Rather than attacking it brutally you begin to jiggle it gently. Two parsecs left! You feel a click, then another, and suddenly it's free! Quickly you pull it back and brake to sublight speed. There's an explosion of light on the viewscreen and then the outside world slowly comes into focus. You are in a zone of giant, tumbling, house-sized rocks.

"Where did these things come from?" you wonder out loud. "The space charts have this sector down as a near void."

"Not a total void," comes the droning voice of your computer. "On the fringes of this zone was the planet Obon. That planet no longer exists. It blew apart a short while ago. What you see is all that remains."

(continued on page 23)

"It's a deal," you say. "What's the riddle."

"Sally has the same number of brothers as she has sisters, but her brother George has twice as many sisters as he has brothers. How many children are there in the kids' family?" says Lea.

"I'm not sure," you say, "but I think the answer is either seven or eight."

If you guess eight, turn to page 112.

If you guess seven, turn to page 83.

"Get back or I'll shoot," you yell.

The alien ignores your warning and continues to reach for the pistol.

You fire point-blank. A blast of energized photons flashes from the pistol. They catch the robot square on the hand. To your surprise—and dismay—the shot fails to bring him down, or even to take off his hand. Instead, the ray bounces off his hand as if it were a mirror. The beam comes screaming back at the speed of light and strikes you squarely.

"Oh, no," you mutter. "I've shot myself. This is ridiculous."

Unfortunately, this is also . . .

The End

You successfully navigate the Stargate and emerge into another universe, and another time. Your tri-space coordinator quickly informs you that you are in the Delta Quadrant, present time.

You look down upon a rocky asteroid and spot the wreck of the tri-clenium cruiser.

"There's our prize," you say. "I'll set up the transporter and we'll beam the crystals aboard."

Before you can reach the transporter you see a chilling sight on your viewscreen. A red and black craft, in the shape of a jellyfish is rising to meet you.

"It's Tentacles Shiver and his outlaw ship, the *Raider's Revenge*," you say to Lorinda. "He means to destroy us. I'll have to get him first."

You quickly lock an SA (Suspended Animation) missile into your torpedo tube. "This will neutralize him," you say.

"With our minds we can create a force field his missiles can't penetrate," says Lorinda.

"Yes, but then I couldn't zap him," you say. "A force field would stop my missiles, too."

If you want the Fuegans to protect you, turn to page 47.

If you want to do without the screens in order to have a free field of fire, turn to page 100.

You realize that your only chance is to bluff. You know that Shiver is a gambler, and you've played some poker, too.

"Go on, Tentacles," you reply. "Blast me. But if you do, it'll be your end, too."

"What are you talking about?" he asks, pulling his tentacle away from the proton launcher.

"I just picked up a load of charged anti-matter from a lab on Darius. I don't have to tell you what happens when protons interact with charged anti-matter. Think it over, Tentacles. You blast me and everything within three light-years will be vaporized."

"It's bluff," you hear one of the raiders say.

"I'm not so sure," says Tentacles. "I want to check this out myself. I'm sure you won't mind if I transport over there, would you?"

If you refuse his request to inspect your ship, turn to page 62.

If you give Tentacles Shiver permission to board, turn to page 49.

You open the door and take a step outside.

"Hey!" you shout. "Who's there? Show yourself!"

The last order was something you quickly wish you'd never made.

For, when your visitor shows herself, you see she's a four-hundred-pound spider. She'd been hiding behind the ship, and now you've blundered into her trap.

You start back up the stairs, but it's too late. The elephant-sized creature has already reached up with one of her six legs and slammed the door shut.

A moment later that same leg reaches out for you.

"Sorry," you say, ducking under the spider's leg. "I'd love to chitchat, but I've got to be going."

Then, leaping from the stairs, you sprint away toward some nearby hills.

Luckily, the spider chooses not to pursue you. But, unluckily, she decides to immobilize your ship by wrapping it up in a thick web.

By nightfall your ship has been mummified and you've been marooned.

"Rats," you mutter, gazing down on your ship. "Those emeralds were nothing but a sophisticated trap to lure me down here, and like a fool I fell right into it. It could be years before I'm rescued. Maybe even centuries."

The End

You take off for the ship, dragging the long rope behind you. You should cut it free, but greed has the better part of you.

"A glue this strong could be worth a fortune," you tell yourself. "All I have to do is get this rope to a lab for analysis and I'm rich."

When you bound up the stairs to your ship, the spiders are still one hundred meters away. You turn around to give the ugly fellows a last look and suddenly trip over the rope you'd been dragging. You land on the sticky web and roll down the stairs. When you hit the bottom you're wrapped up tighter than a mummy.

The spiders, both the size of elephants, soon surround you.

"Listen, fellows," you say, hoping against hope that they understand English. "How'd you like to make a deal? Give me exclusive rights to your web and glues and we'll split the profits fifty-fifty. What do you say? Cut the web and I'll draw up a contract."

You're stunned when one of the spiders responds.

"You make an interesting proposal. We'll talk about it after dinner."

The other spider laughs. You're not certain, but you're afraid you may not be around after dinner to discuss anything.

The End

You dive down to the wreck of the tri-clenium cruiser and hover less than fifty feet above the downed craft.

"Your move, Tentacles," you say. "You can't destroy me now without activating those crystals and frying you and your crew like eggs in a skillet."

"Aye, you're craftier than I thought, mate, but you can't defeat Tentacles Shiver that easily." Then, as he turns to his evil crew, you hear him command, "To the transporter room. We'll board the ship and take it by force!"

Turn to page 46.

Tentacles and his raiders could appear at any moment. Danger or not, you have to enter the cruiser and recover the crystals.

The Hubots wish you luck as you step inside the flimsy wreck. You work your way through the tangled debris, being careful not to touch a thing. Finally you reach the cargo bay, pull back the hatch and gaze down on the di-loid crystals alternately pulsating green and maroon from deep within their velvet-lined storage containers.

"At last, the crystals are mine," you say, leaping into the bay. "I'm rich."

Unfortunately you will also soon be dead. The force of your leap rattles the walls, and in moments the whole ship comes tumbling down like a house of cards. A huge chunk of the fuel tank knocks you out and buries you amidst the crystals you crossed half a galaxy to find.

The End

You ready your photon pistol and stand by as one by one the Space Raiders materialize on your ship. They are the weirdest collection of creatures and misfits you've ever seen. Shiver, a six-foot jellyfish supported by six snakelike tentacles, appears last.

"Every one of us is aboard," he boasts, displaying a golden laser sword. "Prepare to die, my little friend. The crystals are ours."

Then Shiver begins to advance. His laser sword slices through the air, leaving a trail of deadly light. His last words echo in your head: *Every one of us is aboard*. That means his own ship is empty!

You could either try to blast him and his crew with your photon pistol or you could try to reach the transporter and beam over to the deserted *Raider's Revenge*.

Whatever the choice, it had better be fast.

If you decide to shoot Tentacles, turn to page 107.

If you want to try to make a run for the transporter, turn to page 97.

You screw up every ounce of courage you have and walk into the cave.

"Anybody home?" you ask. "I'm a friend."

"I believe that," says a deep voice from the dark depths of the cave. "Step this way so I can get a better look at you."

You're shaking like a nine-point earthquake, but you step into the darkness and look around. As your eyes adjust to the light, you make out a most amazing sight.

It's a sight you'll see, too, when you turn to page 81.

"So, if I guess wrong the Millennium Device will instantly detonate," you think.

You cross your fingers and make your guess. "The height of Mount Everest is 32,504 feet."

The End

But two options remain. While Tentacles and his crew are preparing to board you can try to beam up the crystals with your transporter and then rocket away. Or, you can face the Raiders and try to defeat them once and for all in battle.

If you choose to grab the crystals and escape, turn to page 68.

If you are willing to buck the odds and take on Tentacles Shiver and his crew, turn to page 42.

Lorinda, Gall and the others concentrate their minds and create a force field around the ship. All of Tentacle's missiles explode harmlessly against the force field.

"Keep that field intact," you tell the Fuegans. Then you sweep down over the cruiser, locate the crystals and beam them aboard with your transporter.

"That does it," you tell Lorinda, "my mission is accomplished."

If you choose to head directly for home with the crystals, turn to page 67.

However, if you choose to cancel the force field in order to get a last shot at Tentacles, then turn to page 75.

You open the hatch door and leap to the ground.

"Be careful," you scream to the cub. "Get away from there!"

Unfortunately, your shouts fail to drive the cub away. Indeed, they have the opposite effect. They so startle him that he topples into the sticky tar.

In a flash you snap a branch off a nearby tree and sprint across the clearing to the trapped cub.

"Take it easy," you say. "I'll get you out."

All at once you hear something crashing through the jungle and you wheel about. A huge dinosaur, several stories tall, is lumbering your way. Instinctively you step back, catch your foot on a rock and tumble into the tar. You fight to free yourself, but it seems hopeless. The cub whimpers and catches onto your suit with his claws.

"I'm sorry," you say, looking into the baby's big, sad eyes. "It looks like we're going down together."

WAIT! IT'S JUST POSSIBLE ALL IS NOT LOST. THERE IS HOPE, BUT ONLY IF YOU HELP BY TURNING TO PAGE 60.

You open your transporter channel, clip a tranquilizing round into your pistol and watch as the infamous Space Raider, Tentacles Shiver, materializes before your eyes. From the gelatinous blob with two eyes and a mouth that passes for his head, to the six long tentacles that support his squat, clear body, he's not what you'd call pretty.

You're sorely tempted to knock him out with your tranquilizer and haul him off to the penal colony on Delta Seven. You hesitate only because it would be a cowardly thing to do. You have your honor to worry about, but the future of the galaxy is at stake as well.

If you decide to fire, turn to page 86.

If you elect to hold your fire till Tentacles is aboard, turn to page 52.

Thirty-six hours later the Hubots have eaten their way through to the cargo bay. You step gingerly through the skeleton of the cruiser and glance down on the velvet-lined container that holds the green and maroon crystals.

Suddenly, you hear a shout from one of the Hubots.

"We've picked up Shiver's ship, the *Raider's Revenge,* on our early warning sensors. You'd better clear out before he arrives."

"But I can't leave you fellows here," you say. "He'll cut you into scrap metal."

"Don't worry about us," says a Hubot. "We're made of hardened tritium. Nothing can harm us. Don't be a fool, save yourself."

If you decide to flee, turn to page 61.

If you choose to stay and face Tentacles, turn to page 72.

By dawn the next day the Moltroll has cleaned the skies above Clearview. You flip open your portable locator and quickly find the *Nova Princess*. She's not far away, and so you bid your friends farewell and set off to complete your mission.

You soon reach the remains of the *Princess*. But when you step inside the twisted wreckage, you discover that someone has beaten you there. That someone is a ten-foot giant named Lea.

Turn to page 54.

You've never before been face to face with Tentacles Shiver, though you've seen his picture on plenty of wanted posters throughout the galaxy. He was plenty ugly on those posters, but up close, from the quivering mass of jelly that passes for his head to the six snakelike tentacles he calls his legs, he really looks hideous.

"Now, where are those neutrinos?" he asks, waving a laser sword in your direction.

You thrust out your photon pistol to stop his advance. But then, like lightning, his sword flashes out and strips the gun from your hand.

"Ah ha," he says, placing the sword at your throat. "It seems that you and your ship are now one of my prizes."

(continued on page 53)

Tentacles backs you into the control panel. In desperation you reach back and activate a timer. An alarm sounds and then a deep voice booms from the computer: "Alert! Alert! This ship will self-destruct in ten parsecs. Repeat you have nine parsecs, and counting . . ."

"Only I can punch in the code that will deactivate the destruct order," you say. "Give me that sword and surrender and I'll save our lives."

"You have six parsecs. . . and counting. . ."

"No dice," says Tentacles. "You don't want to die. Stop it for yourself."

"Three parsecs, and counting . . ."

If you choose to deactivate the destruct order, turn to page 91.

If you are willing to let the ship blow, turn to page 79.

You soon learn that Lea is trying to deactivate the Millennium Device, which is contained in a black box in the center of the room.

"I can only deactivate it by solving today's Millennium riddle," she says. "And it's a real toughie."

"Let me try," you say. "I'm a whiz at riddles."

"Not so fast. Remember, I got here first," says Lea. "I'll let you work on the riddle if you agree to split the reward money."

"I'd rather go for all or nothing," you say. "I propose we have a contest. If I win I get the chance at the billion-dram reward. If you win I'll help you solve the riddle and all the money is yours."

"What kind of a contest?" asks Lea.

"I don't care," you say. "I'm pretty good at everything."

If you choose to split the reward, turn to page 34.

If you go for the contest, and all or nothing, turn to page 85.

With Dalox in the lead the Wumpus begin eating their way toward the volcano. Luckily the caterpillars are hungry and you make good progress. But then, around midday, you notice that the digging has stopped.

"What's wrong?" you ask.

"We don't dare venture farther in this direction," says a Wumpus named Melton. "We're on the edge of the Moltroll's territory. We'll have to go around. It'll mean a two-day delay."

"What's a Moltroll?" you ask.

"He's half mole, half vacuum cleaner," explains Dalox. "He roams beneath the surface sucking up everything in his path. If he so much as saw us he'd vacuum us up as if we were specks of dust."

"I'd like to talk to this fellow," you say. "He could come in handy."

"Don't be a fool," says Dalox. "The Moltroll is the deadliest thing on this planet."

"But time is running out," you argue. "The Millennium Device is due to go off in three days. A two-day delay could be fatal."

"So could a brush with the Moltroll," says Melton.

If you choose to contact the Moltroll, turn to page 109.

If you elect to detour around the creature, turn to page 70.

When you open the door you see a red-and-white-striped room filled with balloons and toys. In the middle of all this stands a short, nearly circular man covered with green, bushy hair.

"Greetings," he says. "My name is Professor Chortle. Glad you could come by."

"I'd like to see that diamond you advertised on the door," you say.

"Of course, of course," he says, handing you a photograph. "Here it is."

You look down at the picture. It's a photo of Yankee Stadium, a baseball diamond.

The professor begins to laugh. "Good joke, don't you think?"

You manage a weak smile. "I think I'd better be going," you say.

"Wait a minute," he says, holding out a large, violet flower. "Smell this. It's like nothing else in the galaxy, a rare Lipid from Orion."

If you choose to smell the professor's flower, turn to page 76.

If you decide you've had enough and want to go, turn to page 69.

You turn to run but get only a step or two before you feel something hot, and rough, and sticky wrap itself around your neck.

"Not so fast," you hear a rough, scratchy voice say. "Stick around and let's have a bite to eat."

You get a sinking feeling that the thing around your neck is a tongue, and you're almost certain that the other end is attached to what the Lapto called a "long-tongued one."

"Suffering supernovas," you mutter as the creature begins to reel you in. "Looks like I'm in deep trouble. In fact, unless I'm mistaken, this is . . .

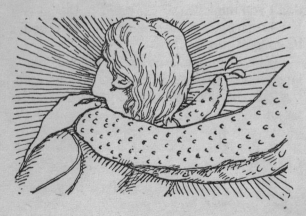

The End

"On the surface," you explain. "The atmosphere of this planet is horribly polluted. We could sure use your help in cleaning it up."

"If there's cleaning to be done I want to do it," says the Moltroll. "How do we get to the surface?"

"Just follow me and my Wumpus friends," you say.

The Wumpus slowly come out of hiding.

"It's okay," you reassure them. "He's agreed to help us."

In short order the Wumpus are again burrowing toward the volcano. The Moltroll brings up the rear, vacuuming up any mess left behind.

By early the next day the heat in the tunnels begins to rise and you realize you are near the volcano.

"Let's go up to the surface," you tell Dalox. "I want to come out on the shores of Crater Lake."

"I think we should dig on for another kilometer," says Dalox, "If we come up now I'm afraid we might hit the volcano."

"And I think we'd miss it," you say. "It's getting hot down here. Please, let's dig up to the top."

If you elect to dig directly to the top, turn to page 93.

If you choose to burrow on for another kilometer before surfacing, turn to page 77.

You glance up at the dinosaur and are relieved to see that he's a Diplodocus, one of the largest, but one of the gentlest, dinosaurs that ever lived. As you recall, they were strictly vegetarians.

"Lunch time!" you shout, waving the branch in your hand. "Come and get it!"

Before long the Diplodocus walks over, drops down his head and takes the leafy end of the branch in his mouth. You literally hold on for your life as the dinosaur lifts you, and the clinging cub, out of the tar. Once free you drop to the ground. The cub gives you a thankful look and then scrambles away.

Go to page 64.

You sprint to your ship with the crystals and lift off, and out of sight, just as the *Raider's Revenge* touches down. You set your screens on optimum magnification and watch as the drama unfolds below you.

To you relief Tentacles ignores the Hubots and heads directly for the wreck with his entire crew.

"What's wrong with those Hubots?" you say to yourself. "I can't understand why they don't escape while they can."

The reason they stayed is soon apparent. For, while the greedy space raiders are clawing their way through the wreck, the Hubots are over at Shiver's ship chewing their way through the *Raider's Revenge*.

"No wonder they stuck around," you say. "Those little guys were hungry!"

By the time Tentacles sees what has happened, his ship is a total loss and the Hubots have blasted away with full stomachs.

"Poor Tentacles," you think. "He wanted to rule the galaxy; now all he has for a kingdom is a worthless hunk of rock."

You smile at the thought and set your course for Hegel, and home.

The End

You've made a big mistake. A real gambler would have strung out the bluff a little longer. Tentacles seizes the opportunity and plays his cards.

"I'll take my chances, pal. If you really had that charged anti-matter aboard, you would have shown it to me. Fire proton torpedoes!"

"Drat," you mutter as the missile zeroes in on your ship. "This has got to be the worst game of cards I ever played."

A moment later you are able to add . . . "And also the last."

The End

"So long," you say to your reptilian friend. "Sorry I can't stay for the party."

You lock in a course for the green planet known as Fuego and blast away from the clearing, leaving the dinosaur very confused.

"Well, I certainly hope Fuego is a friendlier place than Koren," you say to yourself.

Go to page 29.

You spend the remainder of the morning puttering about your ship, gathering supplies and reviewing statistics on the planet's surface. Late that afternoon you hear something banging on the side of the ship. You look out and see a huge, sharp-toothed dinosaur. You run a video image of the beast through the computer and get back the information that the dinosaur is a Tyrannosaurus rex. It also notes that he is extremely dangerous. You shake your head. Koren is not turning out to be very hospitable.

If you decide to leave Koren and explore the other planet, turn to page 63.

If you elect to stay in hopes the dinosaur will leave, turn to page 74.

By observing the Moltroll you become convinced that he's harmless. He's merely obsessed with neatness. That's why he constantly vacuums.

You step from behind the rock, waving the long stick.

"Hey!" you shout. "Stop. I want to talk."

But your words are lost amid the roar of the winds whipping through the tunnel at more than 100 kilometers per hour. Worse yet, the Moltroll doesn't even look up at you. He's too busy cleaning.

Turn to page 66.

As the Moltroll draws nearer it becomes harder to hold out against the tremendous suction. You turn to run, but it's too late. Whoosh! You're suddenly lifted off your feet and sucked toward his great cavernous snout. Instinctively you turn the stick sideways just before you fly into the Moltroll. Whack! The stick is too long to fit into the snout. For a moment the huge beast is stunned. Before he can start up again you're talking a streak.

"Wait, wait a parmin," you say. "I know a place where there is lots of junk for you to clean up."

The Moltroll sniffs the dust off your shoes and eyes you suspiciously.

"Just where is this mess?" he asks.

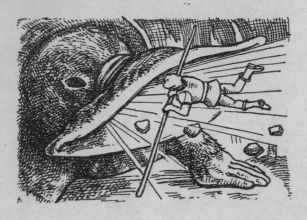

Turn to page 59.

Your force field intact, you slowly begin to accelerate out of the Delta Quadrant. When you reach the speed of light you pass your hand over a green light and jump to hyperspace. When you next check your screen you see that Tentacles and the *Raider's Revenge* are gone.

"Sorry you missed your chance at Tentacles," says Lorinda.

"That's all right," you say. "At least we've kept the crystals out of his evil hands. Anyway, I don't think I've seen the last of that outlaw. I'm sure we'll meet again, somewhere and in some time."

The End

While Shiver and the Raiders are assembling in their transporter room you can scan the tri-clenium cruiser and locate the crystals. Using your transporter beam you bring the crystals on board. Then, before Tentacles can react, you fire your engines and rocket away. You accelerate slowly till you reach the speed of light. Then, you fan your hand over a green sensor and make the jump into hyperspace. You look back, and the *Raider's Revenge* is gone.

You lock in the coordinates for your home base on Hegel and lean back in your chair.

"I guess they'll have a big parade for me when I get back," you say. "Probably be stories about me and Tentacles in the papers, too."

Then, putting your feet up on your desk, you add, "You know, I do think that being a hero is going to be a lot of fun."

The End

"No, thanks, I'm not interested in lipids, or your lame jokes," you tell the professor as you head for the door. "I have things to do."

When you step out the door you make a frightening discovery.

You are not back in the tunnel but, instead, in a house of mirrors. Suddenly the door slams behind you. You take a step and run headlong into one of the hundreds of mirrors that fill the room.

From out of nowhere you hear Chortle laughing. Everywhere you turn you see your reflection. You start to run, but before you've taken three steps you've smashed into another mirror. Again you hear that hideous laugh.

You fear that if you don't break out quickly you might never emerge from this no-fun funhouse.

If you want to try to lower your shoulder and ram your way through the mirrors, turn to page 88.

If you choose to try to blast your way out with your photon pistol, turn to page 90.

"All right," you tell the Wumpus. "We'll take the detour. But please, we must hurry."

And hurry you do. For hours upon hours the giant caterpillars burrow their way through the thick rock beneath Doom. But then, after two days of nonstop digging, the Wumpus begin to slow down. Before long they have stopped altogether. You look around frantically and notice they are all drifting off to sleep.

"Dalox," you say, "you can't go to sleep now."

"I'm afraid we have no choice," she says yawning. "We're going into our cocoon stage. When we reemerge we'll all be butterflies."

"But you can't start changing now," you say. "We're so close."

Dalox's reply is a yawn. Then, closing her big orange eyes, she drifts off into a deep, deep sleep.

In no time the other Wumpus have wrapped themselves in cocoons and gone off to sleep.

"I'm finished," you say to yourself. "I could never find my way out of here and locate the Millennium Device before it explodes. What a terrible development this turned out to be."

Terrible, perhaps, but you don't spend much time worrying about it. The Wumpus yawns have proved contagious and soon you've dropped off to sleep, too.

The End

You fire your thrusters and descend into the dark gray atmosphere that encircles Doom.

"Five parsecs to touchdown," announces the automatic pilot. "Now four, three, two, one."

You feel a slight bump, hear the engines shut down and pull off your safety belt. You are on the surface of Doom and, for the moment, you're alive to experience it.

You clip a small breathing device onto the tip of your nose and step out of the ship and into a gray world filled with dense smoke. It is a lifeless place as far as you can determine.

"I don't think I'd like to meet anything that could thrive in an atmosphere like this," you say.

The words are barely out of your mouth when you hear a frightful roar. You freeze and listen but all you hear is the pounding of your heart. You are about to move on when suddenly it comes again. And now it seems even closer. You're frightened and curious at the same time.

If you decide to call out in order to meet the mysterious creature, turn to page 98.

If you want to stay clear of whatever made the noise, turn to page 116.

"I've been waiting a long time to meet Tentacles Shiver," you tell the Hubots. "I'm not about to run away now."

"You're an idiot," says a Hubot. "You don't stand a chance without armor. You should have left when you had the opportunity."

Too late you realize they are right. Your stubbornness has sealed your fate.

Before long the ferocious Space Raiders are swarming all about you. For a while you and the Hubots fight them to a standstill.

Then suddenly, you feel something gripping your shoulder. You turn your head about and come face to face with the six-foot gelatinous mess known as Tentacles Shiver.

"Sorry we have to meet under such poor circumstances," you hear him say.

And then before you can react, he releases a powerful poison into your shoulder and you feel yourself drifting away into a deep, deep sleep from which you're not sure you'll ever awaken.

The End

By dusk the big beast has toppled over your ship and rendered it totally inoperable. Your computer told you that the dinosaur was dangerous, but it failed to inform you that he was also incredibly persistent. Throughout the night he tears at the thin metallic skin of your ship. By morning he's broken through into your cabin. And by lunch time—well, by lunch time you're his lunch.

The End

A laser beam flashes out from your ship and locks the *Raider's Revenge* in your missile command.

"I've got you now," you say. "The universe has seen the last of Tentacles Shiver!"

"Wrong!" comes the booming voice of Tentacles over your ship-to-ship communicator. "You should have used those screens when they were offered. I've launched a boomerang missile and it's sneaking in from behind. So long, sucker, you'll be blown apart in exactly one parsec.

"I don't believe you for a parsec," you reply.

Then everything goes blank as his boomerang slams into your craft, converting you instantly into neutrinos, electrons and quarks.

The End

You take the flower and lean down to give it a sniff. Just as you do a powerful blast of water shoots into your face.

"Ha, ha, ha," laughs the professor. "Here, now I want you to eat one of the bananas here in the fruit bowl."

"No way, funnyman," you say. "I've had enough of your stupid jokes. I'm leaving."

You turn to go and are surprised to notice that the door you came in through is no longer there. Only two doors lead from the professor's fun factory. One door has a picture of a gun on it. The other door features a strange-looking, bug-eyed puppet.

You're afraid of what awaits you behind either door but you have to get away from that madman.

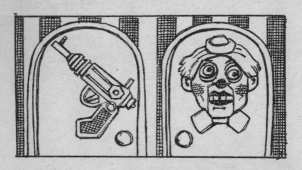

If you want to leave through the gun door, turn to page 87.

If you choose the puppet door, turn to page 96.

You've never experienced such terrible heat. You're certain the volcano will break through the tunnel walls at any moment.

"Hurry," you tell the Wumpus. "I can't breathe."

Just as you are about to pass out you hear a cry from above.

"We've cut through! I can see Crater Lake."

You scramble from the tunnel and emerge on the shores of giant Crater Lake. You never thought you'd be glad to see the polluted skies of Doom again, but the acrid smoke actually feels refreshing to your hot lungs.

You take a drink of the cool lake water and then pull out your photon pistol.

"The volcano is just down the mountain from this lake," you tell Dalox. "I'll blast a hole in the lake and douse the fires below with the floodwaters."

"Maybe you'd better let us eat a hole in the side of the lake," says Dalox. "There's no telling what a big blast could do. Why take a chance at this time?"

If you want the Wumpus to cut through the lake's side, turn to page 99.

If you choose to blast a hole in the lake with your pistol, turn to page 94.

You swing onto the thistle cat and are greatly relieved to find that she's as soft as a newborn kitten. A moment later Chortle has stepped into the room and an instant after that you've swung onto his shoulders.

"Surprise!" you yell, knocking him cold.

Then you dash out of the funhouse and find your friend Dalox amongst a group of the rock-eating Wumpus.

"I'm ready to help," you say.

"Good," says Dalox. "What is your plan?"

"I suggest we dig a hole to the volcano, then flood it with waters from Crater Lake," you say. "That should stop the smoke."

Turn to page 55.

One parsec . . . and those are the last words you will ever hear, for, one parsec later, the ship's hydrogen core implodes and the entire craft is destroyed in a gigantic fireball that reaches out one hundred miles engulfing, and destroying, the *Raider's Revenge*. Though you have given your life, you have destroyed Tentacles Shiver and his ruthless band of Space Raiders. Though you will not live to see it, you will be celebrated throughout the galaxy as one of the greatest heroes in history.

The End

"The answer must be eight," you say. "Seventeen minus nine is eight."

"Wrong," says the Millennium Device. "You fell for a trick question. The answer is nine. If all but nine died, then, of course, nine were left."

"No fair," you say. "Give me another chance."

"Sorry, you blew it," says the Device. "I will detonate in exactly one parmin." Tick, Tick, Tick . . .

CRACK! SMASH! BLAM! Three sledgehammers slam into the *Nova Princess*.

"Those fool alligators think they're going to destroy the *Nova Princes*," you say to yourself. "Little do they realize that it's the *Princess* that's about to destroy them."

Tick . . . tick . . . tick . . .

And about to destroy you, too.

The End

You find yourself gazing into the droopy eyes of the largest caterpillar you have ever seen. As you watch, frozen by fascination and fear, she scoops up a rock with one of her legs, puts it into her sharp-toothed mouth and eats it!

"Relax, my friend. I am a menace to nothing but granite and quartz, both of which I consider delicacies."

(continued on page 82)

"Are you lost here also?" you ask.

"No, no," she says. "I grew up here on Clearview. We were a former earth colony. That is why I know your language."

"Clearview hardly seems a fitting name for this place," you say.

"Our air was once crystal clear," she said. "Then one day a volcano erupted at the base of Crater Lake. It's been polluting our atmosphere ever since. By the way, my name is Dalox and I'm a rock-eating Wumpus."

"Pleased to meet you," you say. "I'm here to find a wrecked ship, the *Nova Princess*. Have you seen it?"

"Until we rid Clearview of the smoke no one will see anything," says Dalox. "Perhaps you will agree to help us cap the volcano. Cutting off the smoke could help us both."

If you choose to help the Wumpus, turn to page 104.

If you think the task is hopeless and go off to find the Princess *on your own, turn to page 15.*

"The answer is seven. There have to be four daughters and three sons. It works out perfectly," you say.

"Correct," says the device. "I am now in a deactivated mode."

You hear a faint whir, a click or two and then silence.

"Mission accomplished," you sigh. "Looks like you and I will soon be rich, Lea."

"And heroes, too," she says. "We've saved a lot of lives today. I wager there will be quite a welcome for you when you return to your home planet."

"That will be nice," you say, "but I hope it's not too big. After everything I've gone through here I'm going to need a good, long rest."

The End

Fifty of the gentle, pig-faced Fuegans crowd into your ship.

"We'll never make it," you say. "There's just too much weight."

"We'll help all we can," says Lorinda. "Our minds can do many things. We'll concentrate on giving you extra power."

You fire your rockets, the creatures concentrate and, miraculously, you slip away from Fuego as smoothly as a bubble being lofted by the wind.

"Wow," you say after you are free of the planet's gravity. "You really can do wonders with your minds. Thanks for the lift."

The Fuegans direct you to a Stargate and urge you to descend into the black hole.

"This should take you to the Delta Quadrant, your original destination," they say.

"And what if it doesn't?" you ask.

"Too bad," says Gall. "We're already under its pull. There's no escape now."

You have no choice. Go to page 36.

Your greed and your ego prove to be your downfall. The contest Lea proposes is arm wrestling.

The ten-foot Lea, who has the strength to match her height, beats you in the wink of an eye—maybe even a little faster.

You live up to your end of the bargain by solving the riddle and thereby deactivating the Millennium Device. But the reward escapes you. You've saved the galaxy, but the time and effort you've put into the mission have worn you out. By early the next day you've blasted off from Doom and are on your way back to Hegel to learn what new adventures await you.

The End

You decide you must neutralize Tentacles while you have the chance. You fire a round of tranquilizing fluid into his quivering body. But instead of finding its mark, it sails through cleanly and lodges in the far wall.

"You fool," comes the voice of Tentacles Shiver. "Did you really think I'd risk sending myself over to your ship. What you just shot was my holographic image."

Suddenly you feel sweat breaking out on your forehead. The bluff is up. You quickly review your remaining options. You can sit still and be blasted into eternity. You can jump into hyperspace (though you doubt you have the power to make the leap to faster-than-light speed ahead of his missiles), or you can dive towards the tri-clenium cruiser and its di-loid crystal cargo. It could cause Tentacles to hold his fire, as a strike on the crystals would be nearly as deadly as a hit on charged anti-matter. The first option is no option at all, so. .

If you want to try to jump to hyper-space for an invisible exit, turn to page 108.

If you want to dive onto the cruiser so he'll hold his fire, turn to page 40.

You open the door and step into a large room. A dozen other people are already there, crouched behind a pile of broken furniture.

"What is this place?" you ask a worried-looking man.

"A shooting gallery. It's one of Chortle's amusement games," he replies.

"That sounds like fun," you say, pulling out your pistol. "What do we shoot at?"

"We don't shoot at anything. We get shot *at*," he says.

It's then that you notice a row of people standing at the far end of the room behind a long counter. They all have laser weapons—and they're all aimed at you.

"Oh, boy," you hear one of them remark. "Chortle just put a fresh target in there. Let's see how fast that kid can move."

Zing! A blast of photons knocks the gun out of your hand. You duck down behind a broken couch and wonder what the life expectancy of a human target is.

The End

You lower your shoulder and crash into the mirrors. The mirrors give way and you find yourself in a large room. In the center of the room you see a surprising sight. Its the *Nova Princess!* Three tall, alligator-faced creatures are standing near the wreck with large sledge-hammers. Above the spaceship is a sign that says: WRECK THE WRECK! THREE WHACKS FOR A QUARTER.

"It's another one of Chortle's sick arcade games," you say. "I've got to get to the Millennium Device before those jokers destroy it."

You dash into the *Nova Princess* and find the black box that holds the deadly Millennium Device. You touch the box and a voice speaks to you: "In order to defuse me you must solve this riddle—a farmer had seventeen cows. All but nine died. How many were left?"

If the answer is eight, turn to page 80.

If the answer is nine, turn to page 106.

"We understand," says Lorinda. "We wouldn't want to see your ship crash."

She then shows you an ancient book that contains the location of a number of Stargates in the vicinity. You pick one that looks as if it can lead you to your original destination, the Delta Quadrant.

After saying your good-byes you head directly for the Stargate, a huge, rotating black hole. Once in orbit above the hole you cut your engines and let yourself be sucked into the swirling void. For what seems like an eternity, and well could be, you're buffeted about by tremendous gravitational forces. At last, just as you think your ship will be torn apart, you're shot out of the hole and into a universe that looks totally unfamiliar. The sky is a brilliant white, and where the stars should be there's nothing but black dots. It looks just like a photographic negative. As far as you can determine you're on the backside of your own universe. A feeling of panic surges over you. You're stuck in an alien universe and you don't have the foggiest idea of how to escape.

The End

You pull out your photon pistol and level it at a mirror. The moment you fire you realize you've made a terrible mistake. Since photons are nothing but bullets of light they don't penetrate the mirrors, they reflect off of them. Zing! A blast of photons ricochets off the mirror and comes screaming back, only to bounce off another mirror. Zing! Off it comes again at the speed of light. You hit the floor, roll over and watch as the light whips around the room, blasting from mirror to mirror.

Pinned to the floor, you have no choice but to lie in place and watch the light show unfold. There is no escape. If you rose you'd be shot down instantly—by your own pistol.

The End

Death is not something you had planned for that afternoon, so you dive for the control panel and punch in the deactivate code X-1-T.

Destruct deactivated, says the computer. *Operations now normal.*

You sigh and look over at Tentacles. He seems as calm as a Malium Mouse.

"No more tricks," he says. "Next time you try anything like that I'll cut you into atoms. Now, where are those neutrinos?"

Two doors lead from the control room. One leads to a Corolite freezer filled with Zeon bricks, kept solid by temperatures approaching absolute zero. The other leads to a passageway that connects to the rest of the ship.

If you choose to direct Tentacles to the freezer door, turn to page 115.

If you choose to send him down the passageway, turn to page 118.

After checking with the Intergalactic Encyclopedia in the ship's library you are able to tell the device that the correct answer is 29,028 feet.

"You're right," says the device. "I will now officially deactivate myself."

As you watch, a puff of smoke comes out of the device, and then it falls silent.

"At last, the galaxy is safe," you say to yourself.

You've still got to get off Doom, but that's something you can worry about later. Right now you want to celebrate the deactivation in the ship's kitchen. As you recall there were two more mouth-watering double burgers in the Eternal Warm Oven—and some Tasty Time French fries as well.

The End

You direct the Wumpus to dig directly to the surface. Though it grows hotter you are not discouraged. You expect heat this near the volcano. You only hope you are also near the lake.

Then, all of a sudden, one of the newly cut walls begins to glow red.

"The volcano!" yells the Moltroll. "She's breaking through!"

A moment later lava begins spilling into the tunnel.

"Suffering Supernovas!" you exclaim. "I am sorry. Looks like I decided to have us surface a little early."

The Moltroll and the Wumpus appear none too pleased with your apology, but there is nothing they can do about it because, after all, this is . . .

The End

"I can handle this," you say, setting the photon pistol for maximum damage. "Watch this."

You direct a beam of highly charged photons into the side of the lake. Because of the thick haze you can't see exactly what you hit. This turns out to be most unfortunate. That's because you strike a deposit of highly unstable chelsenium. The blast triggers a chain reaction that instantaneously melts the entire side of the crater, including the spot you've been standing on.

You hear a tremendous roar as the water floods out of the lake, sweeping you along with it. You grab hold of a huge root and pull yourself to a stand. Like a surfer on a tidal wave you speed toward shore. Shore, however, is not a sandy beach but a raging volcano.

"Maybe the waters will turn the volcano into a huge hot tub," you say to yourself. "Wouldn't that be nice."

It would be nice. But it's not reality. What you're heading for is not some surfer's fantasy. What you're heading for is a massive, active volcano.

The End

You walk into the puppet room and are astounded by what you see. Hanging from the ceiling are hundreds of puppets of different shapes and sizes. Almost every intelligent life form in the galaxy is represented. What is most surprising, though, is not the variety of puppets, but the fact that all of them are alive!

You shake your head and are about to leave when all at once you feel yourself being lifted to the ceiling. Ropes have somehow been attached to your body.

"At last," you hear the professor say, "I've got a human puppet. Something I've always wanted."

You've got better things to do than hang from the ceiling, so you pull out your laser knife and reach up to cut the ropes. Just before you make the first slice you look down and make a horrible discovery. The floor has disappeared. Below you is nothing but blackness. The bottom could be three meters away, or it could be a zillion.

If you decide to go ahead and cut the ropes and take your chances in the pit, turn to page 101.

If you choose to remain suspended for the time being, turn to page 110.

"Hold it right there," you say, waving your pistol at Tentacles and his crew. "I'm not afraid to use this."

You keep up a steady stream of threats as you back into the transporter room.

Before throwing the switch that will transport you to the *Raider's Revenge,* you pull a green crystal from a wall panel and smash it to the floor.

"This craft will self-destruct in three parmins," you say.

Moments later you find yourself aboard the empty *Raider's Revenge.* A scan of the triclenium wreck pinpoints the crystals. Using Shiver's transporter beam you bring the crystals on board and rocket away. You look back just in time to see your old ship destruct in a flash of yellow and red.

You lock in a course for Hegel and sigh. You've lost your ship, but you've rid the galaxy of Tentacles Shiver. You consider it a fair trade. Then, smiling, you remember the crystals you have just salvaged. Soon, you realize, you will not only be a hero, but a very rich one, too.

The End

You take a deep breath and call out, "Anyone there?"

There is a moment's silence and then an excited reply. "Yes, yes, stay there. I'm coming."

A moment later a giant, monkeylike creature emerges from the murk. You recognize him as a Lapto, from the purple planet of Laptos.

"At last I've been rescued," he cries. "I've wandered this planet for years looking for my ship."

The Lapto explains that others are also lost on the planet's surface. "The smoke is so disorienting that anyone leaving his ship becomes almost immediately lost," he says.

"You're safe now," you say. "Come, I'll take you to my ship. It's not far. It's just over—"

Suddenly you're not quite sure which direction it's in.

If you elect to turn right, go to page 111.

If you elect to turn left, go to page 113.

The Wumpus splash into the lake and go to work weakening the wall above the volcano. Before long they've got it looking like a rocky hunk of Swiss cheese.

"It should go any moment now," says Dalox, emerging from the water. "We'd best stand back."

You step back just as water begins to spill out of the side of the huge lake. A parsec later the whole side collapses and a hundred-meter wall of water cascades down on the volcano, sending up a tremendous cloud of steam as it meets the red-hot lava.

For nearly an hour the flood continues. When it is all over you look down on a wondrous sight. A new Crater Lake has formed in the volcano. Best of all, smoke is no longer pouring into the atmosphere of Doom.

"All right," you tell the Moltroll. "Go to work. Vacuum up these skies. I've got a spaceship to find."

Now go to page 51.

You program in the coordinates of the *Raider's Revenge* and launch your SA missile. An instant later it finds its mark, wrapping the outlaw vessel in a cloak of lightning. When, at last, the electricity subsides, the *Raider's Revenge* is left dead in space. Your missile has put the ship, and everyone on board, in a frozen state of suspended animation.

"We'll leave her here as a permanent exhibit," you tell Lorinda. "Everyone passing this way will surely want to stop and tour the inside of a real Raider's ship. Looks like I've made Tentacles famous. He may not know it, but he's about to become the hottest tourist attraction this side of the photon ride at Quasarland!"

The End

You slice through the rope with your laser knife and drop into the void. After a short fall you land on a hard, rock floor. While you're picking yourself up the lights suddenly come on, and you see you're in a windowless room surrounded by high, polished, steel walls.

"Hello," says a squat little man in clown makeup who is sitting in a corner. "Welcome to the dungeon of bad jokes."

"Bad jokes?" you say.

"Yeah, like, why did the android cross the road? To get to the other side, of course! And, why did the Martian throw the butter out the window? To see the butterfly!" says the clown.

"Stop, stop," you beg. "Those bad jokes are killing me."

"That's just it," chuckles the clown. "That's why this place is a dungeon. You're going to have to listen to these for the rest of your days. Here's a real bad one. What hangs from a tree and goes buzz? An electric prune!"

"Stop, stop," you cry. "I can't stand any more."

"Too bad," laughs the clown. "By the way, have you heard about the crazy robot who . . ."

The End

You take a tiny bite out of the branch. It tastes delicious! You take another bite then another, and another. You can't remember a meal being so good. You don't look up till you're full; when you do, you see a horrified look on the Lapto's face.

"Your arms!" he says.

You look down and are struck speechless. Your arms are sprouting colorful feathers. You touch your face and find your mouth becoming a beak. When at last you find your voice, it's too late. By then all you can do is squawk and say a few simple phrases such as, "Hello. How are you?" and one other that you repeat over and over, "Polly doesn't want to be a parrot! Polly doesn't want to be a parrot! Polly doesn't want to . . ."

The End

You don't want to hurt the Moltroll, so you set your pistol on *Stun*. When the creature is about twenty meters away you step out from behind your rock and raise the gun. With the air roaring down the tunnel at 100 kilometers per hour, it's difficult to aim. Luckily the Moltroll is so busy with his housekeeping that he doesn't seem to notice you.

You battle the blowing dust and dirt, trying to get a bead on the advancing creature. The winds increase to a shriek.

Whoosh! The pistol is sucked out of your hands and into the gaping snout of the Moltroll. You grab a boulder and hold on for all you're worth. Whoosh! There go your shoes and socks!

"Hey! Hey!" you scream, trying, hopelessly, to be heard over the roar of the winds.

The Moltroll doesn't even look up. He's too busy tidying things up. Unfortunately, one of the things to be tidied up is you. And, before you know it, whoosh! There goes you.

The End

"I'd be glad to help," you say. "Where do we start?"

"First I want you to meet the rest of my people," she says. "Follow me."

Dalox takes you into a tunnel that leads out of the rear of the cave. After a short walk you emerge into a large, well-lit cavern filled with more of the giant caterpillars.

"Our friend here is going to help us put out the volcano," says Dalox.

"Wonderful," says a Wumpus named Melton. "What is your plan?"

"Dig a hole to the volcano, then flood it with waters from Crater Lake," you say.

"A simply brilliant plan," says Melton. "Let us begin at once."

Turn to page 55.

Grabbing the bee turns out to be a very shocking experience. One hundred volts of electricity ripples through your body. Your hands pop open and you drop away into the darkness. After a short fall you land on a seat in a little open-air train chugging its way through a dimly lit tunnel.

"Looks like I've landed on one of Chortle's amusement rides," you say.

The seat next to you is occupied by a thin-faced man in a stovepipe hat.

"Where is this thing going?" you ask.

"Nowhere," he replies. "That's what the ride is called: Journey to Nowhere."

"Doesn't it ever stop?"

"Of course not, that would ruin the fun," he replies.

"But I don't want to stay on forever," you say.

"Sorry, unless you're heading for the same place as we are, you're out of luck," says the man.

"And what place is that?" you ask.

"I told you," he laughs. "We're all going nowhere. And now, of course, so are you."

The End

"Nine, of course," you say. "If all but nine died, then there had to be nine left."

"Absolutely correct," replies the taped voice inside the Millennium Device. "I am now deactivated."

You hear a series of whirs and clicks, and then the box falls silent.

You smile. You've saved the galaxy from destruction. You still must get off Doom, but you reason that that will not be too hard. After what you've accomplished, any task will seem easy by comparison.

The End

"You may get me Tentacles, but you'll pay a heavy price," you warn the advancing monster. "I've got this pistol set for a dimensional blast. Another step and I'll shoot you into the sixth dimension."

He answers with a growl and lunges at you with his sword. You step back and fire. A burst of photons freezes him in place. Then, out of nowhere, a mirror spins into view, captures the infamous Raider as if he were a reflection, then spins away into the dimension from which it came.

A moment later the rest of the crew overwhelms you. You realize you're done for, but with the end of Shiver his gang is broken. You smile as you slump to the floor, secure in the knowledge you've gone out as a galactic hero.

The End

You slam your controls full-thrust forward. The craft shudders and begins to accelerate toward the speed of light. You've caught Tentacles by surprise. You've already leaped beyond the reach of his torpedoes. But, unfortunately, you haven't leaped beyond the reach of physics. The strain of the acceleration is too great. Your ship flies apart in a million pieces and you find yourself flung into empty space. With no oxygen you have maybe a minute to live. You look back on the planet and on the *Raider's Revenge*. In possession of the crystals, Shiver will rule the galaxy. To you, death is preferable to slavery under the Space Raiders.

The End

A Wumpus chews his way through a wall and into a large tunnel belonging to the dreaded Moltroll. In the distance you hear a high, whining sound. "That's him," says Dalox.

The Wumpus draw back and you crouch down behind a large boulder.

As the creature approaches, the air begins to rush past you. You brace yourself and watch as the massive mole appears. He's as big as a house, with a huge snout for a nose. As he moves through the tunnel the nose sweeps up everything before it.

You have to get his attention, but you're not certain how. His vacuum is making so much noise your shouts would never be heard. You could either thump him on the head with a large tree root that's not far away or stun him with your photon pistol.

If you choose to use the pistol, turn to page 103.

If you prefer the tree root, turn to page 65.

After hanging about for a while you decide that the life of a professional puppet is not for you. Before long a plan takes shape in your mind, and you begin to put it into effect. You reach up and cut yourself free with your knife. However, instead of dropping to the pit you swing onto the puppet next to you. From there you swing onto another puppet and another as you make your way toward the door. Your plan is a simple one. You'll lie in wait and jump Chortle the next time he steps into the room.

At last only one row of puppets separates you from the door. However, the puppets look absolutely untouchable. You are almost certain one is an electric bee. The shock of touching such a creature would probably drop you into the pit. The other fellow looks like a thistle cat, whose fur is sharp and highly poisonous. You could be mistaken, though; it's been a long time since you've seen one this close.

Suddenly you hear Chortle's footsteps. You have to make your decision quickly!

If you decide to swing onto the electric bee, turn to page 105.

If you choose to take your chances by grabbing the thistle cat, turn to page 78.

You strike off toward what you hope will be the ship, but, after a few hours, you realize you are hopelessly lost.

After stumbling about all day, you come to a forest of tree-sized mushrooms.

"Are these things edible?" you ask your Lapto companion.

"Most of them are fine, but some of them are transformational," he says.

"You mean they can turn a person into another animal?" you ask?

"That's right, so be careful what you eat," he says.

You break off a branch and eye it hungrily.

'If you decide to take a bite, turn to page 102.

If you don't eat it, turn to page 114.

"The correct answer is eight!" you say confidently.

"*Incorrect,*" replies the device. "You are totally wrong."

"Then the answer is seven!" you say hurriedly.

"Too late," answers the Millennium Device. "In three hours and three parmins I will detonate."

"Hold on, can't we work something out?" you say.

"In three hours and now two parmins I will detonate," drones the device.

You sigh and sink to the floor of the *Nova Princess*.

"It's stupid to argue with a machine," you tell Lea.

"Yeah," says Lea. "Stupid just like your answer to the riddle."

The End

You swing left and resume the search for your ship. All day long you trudge across the rocky wastes of Doom. Late in the day you come to a steep cliff and discover two large caves.

"We'd better get out of here," says the Lapto. "It's the home of the long-tongued ones, and of the sharp-toothed ones, too."

"And who are they?" you ask.

"The sharp-toothed ones are rock eaters," says the Lapto. "They won't harm us, but the long-tongued ones aren't so particular. I've lost many friends near these caves."

"But I need to find the wreck of the *Nova Princess*," you say. "Maybe the creatures here know where it is. I've got to at least ask."

"Stay if you wish," says the Lapto in a quavering voice. "I'm leaving. I suggest you do the same."

If you decide to enter the cave and talk to the creatures there, turn to page 44.

If you decide to run away like your Lapto friend, turn to page 58.

Leaving the Lapto behind, you stumble away in search of something, anything, to eat.

Suddenly your nose begins to twitch. You detect an odor you haven't smelled since your last visit to earth.

"Mmmmmm," you sigh. "It's a Tasty Time double burger. That smell could be coming from only one place, the *Nova Princess*. She's from earth."

You follow your nose till you come to the wreck of the *Princess*. A double burger is still sizzling in the Eternal Warm oven. You gulp it down and then locate the Millennium Device, a black box containing a bomb powerful enough to wipe out a third of the galaxy. The device senses your presence and speaks: "If you wish to deactivate me you must answer today's question. What is the height of the tallest mountain on planet earth, Mount Everest?" Is it 29,028 feet or 32,504 feet?"

If you can find a reference book in the ship's library you'll want to look up the correct answer because the wrong answer will immediately detonate the device.

If you think the answer is 29,028, turn to page 92.

If you believe the answer to be 32,504, turn to page 45.

"They're behind that door," you say. "That's my storage bay."

"Aye," says Shiver, unlatching the Corolite freezer door. "I do believe I'll peek inside and see those neutrinos."

The instant the door is opened Tentacles is enveloped in a blast of super-cooled air. In a wink he freezes solid as a statue in the minus-363-degree air.

With the giant jellyfish immobilized you lock a tractor beam onto the crystals in the wreck below and pull them aboard.

Then, before the outlaws aboard the *Raider's Revenge* have a chance to react, you blast away with your frozen prisoner.

"Sorry if you are cold," you remark to Tentacles. "But don't worry, they'll thaw you out on Delta Seven. There's a prison there where I'm sure they'll keep you nice and cozy and warm."

The End

Your only thought is to get as far away from the monster as possible. For more than an hour you run blindly through the smoky wasteland of Doom. Finally, when you are sure you are safe, you pause to rest.

"Once I catch my breath I'll double back to the ship," you say. But even as you speak a horrible feeling of dread is creeping over you. The ship! You have no idea where it is. You can barely see your hand in front of your face. Finding your ship will be difficult at best.

And at worst it will be impossible. This place isn't called the Planet of Doom for nothing. You may very well be destined to eternally wander the surface of Doom, eternally searching for your ship or at least for a friendly Missing Person's Bureau or even for a lost and found.

The End

"Tentacles," you say. "I'm breaking off. The crystals are yours."

"Wise move," you hear Tentacles reply. "You're a smart kid."

The words flatter you, but they're as big a lie as his promise to let you go. For already you're in his sights. And already the proton torpedo that seals your fate is on its way.

They didn't teach you about spineless characters like Mr. Shiver in flight school. Too bad, because now, with the missile only moments away, it's much too late to learn the lesson.

The End

You open the door and race down the passageway with Tentacles close behind. Suddenly, in a moment of inspiration, you throw open the emergency exit hatch. Instantly, the vacuum in space starts to suck everything out of the ship. You grab hold of an iron bar on the bulkhead and hold on against the raging torrent of air. Tentacles bellows, drops to his stomach and begins sliding toward the open exit. Just before he is sucked out one of his tentacles reaches out and grabs hold of your waist. The added weight of that giant jelly fish is too much and you lose your grip. Within moments you find yourself waltzing away into the cosmos in the many arms of Mr. Tentacles Shiver.

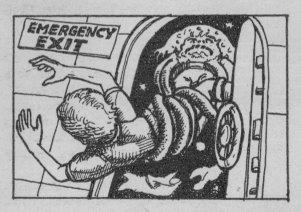

The End

About the Author and Illustrator

STEPHEN MOOSER was born and grew up in Fresno, California. He received a bachelor's degree in motion pictures and a master's degree in journalism from U.C.L.A. He worked as a reporter and filmmaker before writing children's books. Mr. Mooser is also a former treasure hunter; he has searched for pirate treasure in Panama and outlaw treasure belonging to Butch Cassidy in Utah. "Though I found no major part of these treasures," the author says, "parts of my adventures have found their way into my books."

Mr. Mooser lives in Laguna Beach, California, with his wife, Etta, and their two children, Chelsea and Bryn.

GORDON TOMEI studied at the School of Visual Arts and the Art Students League in New York City. He began his art career as a "fine artist," holding gallery exhibitions in the New York area. Three years ago, Mr. Tomei moved into the exciting and interesting world of commercial illustration, which he now prefers, and recently began illustrating children's books.

Mr. Tomei lives in Centerport, Long Island, with his wife, Lorna, who is also a well-known illustrator of children's books.